12/04

O9-ABI-252

The Littlest Magi

Written by Chris Auer

Illustrated by Bruce Eagle

Zonderkidz

Zonderkidz

The children's group of Zondervan

www.zonderkidz.com

The Littlest Magi
ISBN: 0-310-70663-7
Copyright © 2004 by Chris Auer
Illustrations copyright © 2004 by Bruce Eagle

Requests for information should be addressed to:
Zonderkidz, Grand Rapids, Michigan 49530

Library of Congress Cataloging-in-Publication Data

Auer, Chris, 1955-
    The Littlest Magi : a Christmas Tale / by Chris Auer.-- 1st ed.
        p. cm.
    Summary: The smallest servant in King Herod's household follows the Magi and the star to a stable in Bethlehem, where he discovers a new kind of king, in whose kingdom the great and the small will stand side by side.
    ISBN 0-310-70663-7 (hardcover)
    [1. Jesus Christ--Nativity--Fiction. 2. Magi--Fiction. 3. Household employees--Fiction.] I. Title.
PZ7.A9113Li 2004
[E]--dc22
                                                                  2004000493

Zonderkidz is a trademark of Zondervan.

Editor: Gwen Ellis/Amy DeVries
Art Direction and Design: Laura M. Maitner

Printed in China
04 05 06/HK/4 3 2 1

At times being small was a good thing. Jacob could slip in and out of shadows, climb and hide, crawl and jump, and get to places that no one else could reach.

One night he saw a beautiful star. He wanted to see it better, so he climbed to the very top of the very tallest tower of King Herod's palace.

When Jacob looked at the star, he didn't feel so sad or small or unwanted. Instead he felt happy and warm and wonderful. And he couldn't be sure … he wasn't positive … but he thought he heard singing up in the clouds. He couldn't quite catch the words, but the song made his heart beat faster.

He wanted more than anything to feel loving arms around him and hear kind words whispered to him as he fell asleep each night. Instead Jacob was kicked and teased for smelling like old onions and melon rinds.

No one knew the secret hiding places and passages in King Herod's palace better than Jacob. When the cook's son went after him with a stick one afternoon, Jacob slipped into the shadows, ducked down a hallway, climbed a wall, and hid in the rafters above the throne room.

Far below him some men bowed to Herod.

"We're looking for the new king," they explained. "We followed his star here."

A new king! So that's what the star means, thought Jacob, smiling.

"A new king!" said Herod. He did not want a new king. After all, wasn't he the king? "Go and search him out," he declared. "And then come back and tell me where he is so I may go and honor him, as well."

I will look for him, too, Jacob decided. He slipped out of the palace and into the strangers' campsite. He hid himself inside a rolled-up rug and waited.

How can anyone so small have so much dirt on him?" laughed the cook's son.

It was not easy to be the smallest person in a large palace, but Jacob was. As the smallest and least important of King Herod's servants, it was his job to take the kitchen garbage away in a big cart. It was hard work but Jacob didn't mind. He was proud to be helping.

"After all," he said, "it is the king's garbage."

Jacob didn't have any parents or brothers or sisters to look out for him and take care of him. He tried not to think about that, for it made him sad.

For Jane, who knows all about faith and courage.
—C.A.

For Jessica, Kevin, and Cris
—B.E.

As the strangers prepared to leave, they looked out and wondered what Herod would do. They wondered if they had done the right thing by going to see him.

"A king does not like to hear that there is another king," said one.

"Especially King Herod," said a second.

"Yes, but even a king has to listen when God speaks," said a third. He lifted a rolled-up carpet from the ground. "This gets heavier every time we move it," he grunted as he slung it on the back of a camel.

Soon the caravan was under way. From inside the carpet, a pair of eyes watched the palace get smaller and smaller. Jacob fell asleep full of hopes about the new king.

A quick snap sent Jacob flying out of his hiding place and onto the tips of some very elegant shoes. But the wise faces that looked down at him were more amused than angry.

"What do we have here?" one of them asked.

The Wise Men shared their dinner with Jacob near the fire. Jacob told them his story, and then they told him their story. Each of the wise men explained how he had seen the star and set off to follow it many weeks before.

"My friends called me foolish," said one.

"Mine tried to stop me," said another.

"But we didn't have a choice," said the one with the curly beard. "The real foolishness is to ignore God's voice."

As Jacob looked up at the star, he wondered what God's voice sounded like and if he would ever hear it.

The next day the Wise Men searched a little village for the new king.

"A king? Here? In this dusty place?" laughed some of the people.

Jacob did wonder about that, but the wise men kept looking. Then, in a little house on the edge of town, they found him.

Jacob blinked back tears of disappointment.

This doesn't look like the house of a king, he thought. Yet his friends knelt in front of the baby and gave him their gifts.

The baby's mother, Mary, seemed to know what Jacob was thinking.

"God is doing something new," she whispered. "It is time for the world to have a different kind of king. This baby will not look down at you from a palace but will open the door to a kingdom where everyone is loved and where everyone will live in peace with one another."

Jacob wondered how such a thing could be true.

W e have found
our new king,"
said one of the wise men.
"But now it is time to go home."
"How will you return?" asked
Joseph, the baby's earthly father. "King
Herod is not a man you can trust."
"I had a dream," said the one with the gray
beard. "The God of Israel warned me not to go back
the way we came."
Jacob looked down as the others nodded in agreement. He was
suddenly sad. "I have to go home, too," he said very quietly.
"Did you find what you were looking for, Jacob?" asked Mary.
Jacob held the little baby in his arms. "A new kind of king…," he
said softly.
"And a new kingdom, where the great and the small will stand
side by side," Mary added.
Jacob took Jesus' tiny hand in his own, and for a moment he did not feel
quite so small.

Jacob slipped back into the palace. For once it was good to be small, for no one even noticed he had been gone. He had a lot to think about now when he took away the garbage in the big cart.

"What I looked for and what I found were very different," he said to the scruffy cat that followed him. "But I'm glad I looked."

The cat rubbed against Jacob's leg and purred.

"I'm glad I looked, because I found something better," he realized. "Imagine, a kingdom where even someone like me is important!"

For now Jacob still lived in a palace with an angry king. If he closed his eyes, though, he could still feel Joseph and Mary hugging him good-bye. He could still see the way the baby Jesus smiled at him. There was something about that little family that reminded him of the brightness of the special star, and it somehow made him braver.

Jacob needed to be brave, for late one night he heard two soldiers talking about the children in Bethlehem.

"There can only be one king in Israel," said the soldier with the cruel face as he sharpened his sword.

Jacob was afraid for his friends. He slipped into the shadows, crept over a rooftop, slid down a tree, hurried away from the palace, and ran all the way to Bethlehem.

Early the next morning Jacob blurted out his story to Joseph and Mary. They were not surprised by what he said.

"I was visited by an angel in a dream," Joseph explained. "The angel warned me that I must flee to Egypt with Jesus and Mary."

Jacob's eyes went wide with wonder.

"We have much to do. Can you help us, Jacob?"

Jacob nodded.

That night Jacob led Mary and her precious baby through the darkened streets of Bethlehem. If anyone knew how to slip in and out of shadows quietly or how to find a hidden alley, it was Jacob. They didn't speak as they moved through the silent streets.

Joseph was waiting for them outside the gates. He had taken the donkey and left the city earlier that day so no one would notice and try to follow them.

"A group of soldiers rode by just after sundown," whispered Joseph. Jacob and the little family hurried away from Bethlehem as quickly as possible.

Jacob wanted to go with them to Egypt, but Joseph and Mary felt it was too dangerous. At a well, where the road split, Joseph talked to the head of a caravan that was traveling north.

"Jacob, you can go with these people," said Joseph when he returned. "Mary and I think it is no longer safe for you in Herod's palace. We have family up north, and I've made arrangements to get you there. They'll take good care of you."

"Will you do something for me, Jacob?" asked Mary. "Will you tell my family all that has happened? Will you tell them we will return to Nazareth when it is safe?"

Jacob agreed. He then took Jesus from Mary and kissed him good-bye.

"I never had a brother," he said.

"You have one now," Mary replied.

There was sadness and happiness when they said good-bye, but deep inside, where the truth of the new kingdom burned as bright as Jesus' star, Jacob knew that he would see his friends again. There was still another reason for Jacob's big smile as he rode atop the camel heading north. The words Mary and Joseph left him with echoed in his head.

"Remember everything you've seen and heard," Joseph told him. "For the day will come when other people will rejoice to hear the story of Jesus and his birth."

"And listen carefully for God's voice in all that you do," said Mary. "Sometimes he speaks through a star, sometimes through the songs of the angels, sometimes through the quiet tears of an old man. And sometimes his voice is the voice of a little boy."